The Barber's Cutting Edge

Story by Gwendolyn Battle-Lavert
Pictures by Raymond Holbert

Children's Book Press
San Francisco, California

"Hey! Rashaad my man! I just called your number. Hop into my chair. What'll it be today — college cut, shag, fade clark, or gumby?" jived Mr. Bigalow. "Or do you want my SPECIAL DELUXE?"

The barbershop was full of customers. Little boys. Big boys. Young men. And old men. There was even one girl there waiting to get her hair cut. They were all waiting for the best barber in town.

"Why, with the extension of my hand, I can sculpt and create. So, what you want today?"

"I'll take your SPECIAL DELUXE," said Rashaad.

"What you got up your sleeve today, my man?" said Mr. Bigalow. He put a clean towel around Rashaad's neck. "Looks to me like you got a new vocabulary list."

"I bet you don't know the meanings!" challenged Rashaad.

"My man, you *know* that words are what I've always been good at."

"Well, I'll call them out to you. Let's see if you can tell me the meanings. Okay?"

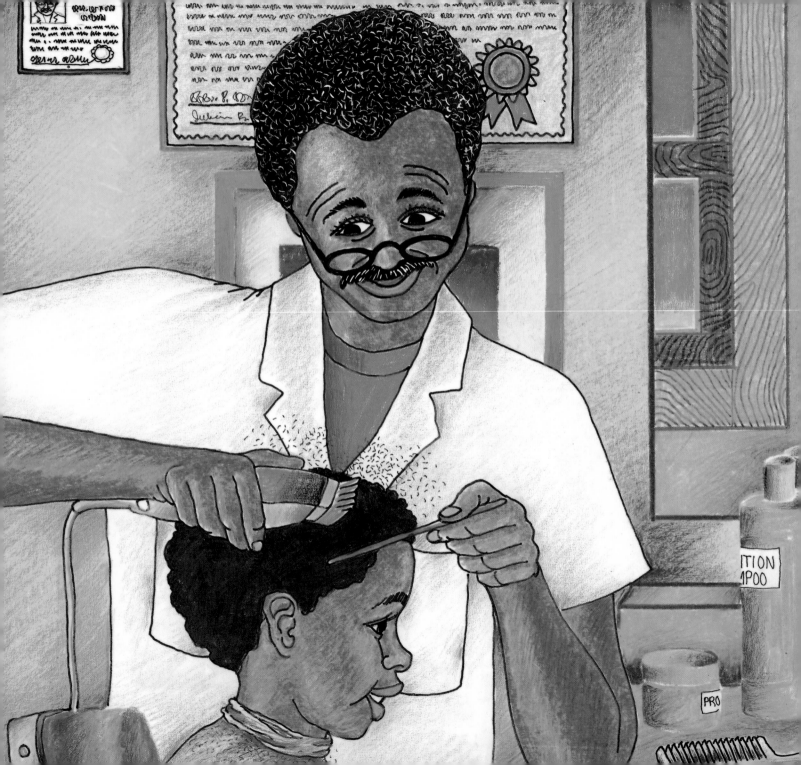

"Lay 'em on me!" said Mr. Bigalow. His high-powered stainless steel clippers started across Rashaad's head.

ZOOOOOOOOOOM!

Rashaad was sure he would be able to stump Mr. Bigalow. These were hard words. He had needed help with them. His Daddy had called them out to him. His Mama had made him write the definitions four times. Then his sister had made him repeat the definitions five times.

"All right, you asked for it!" said Rashaad. "What does BEWILDERMENT mean?"

Mr. Bigalow didn't even pause. "Rashaad my man, this is so easy. BEWILDERMENT is a state of being puzzled or confused."

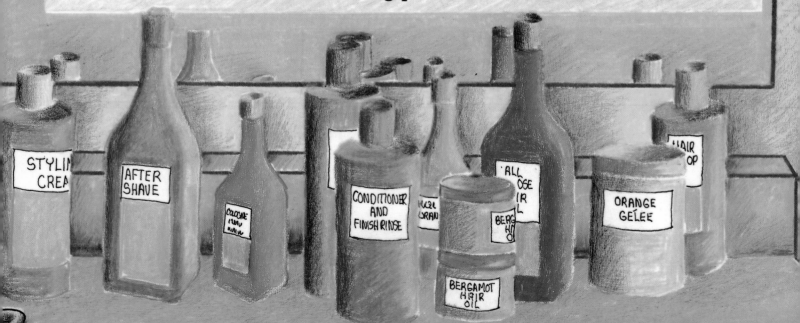

"Ah, man! I see you're hot today," said Rashaad. "Well, you won't get this one. What is the meaning of ABOLISH?"

"Well now, the meaning of ABOLISH is to cancel or undo," said Mr. Bigalow.

"Mr. Bigalow, that word was just too easy," sighed Rashaad. "Try this one for size! What's the meaning of IDIOSYNCRATIC?"

"Do *you* know the meaning of this word?" asked Mr. Bigalow in mock surprise.

Rashaad tried hard to remember it, but he couldn't. "No, I don't know it," he admitted, twisting around in his seat.

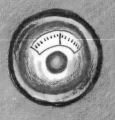

"Hold still, my man!" said Mr. Bigalow. "You keep moving around like that and you're gonna walk outa here with a plug cut out of your hair. Now, how in the world do you expect me to know the meaning if you don't? But no problem. I know this word."

MAVERICKS
GAME
SCHEDULE

Mr. Bigalow's clippers came to a sudden halt.

"Mm mm mm! I don't believe this. Rashaad my man, these clippers need some adjusting. This little screw just won't stay in. I thought I fixed this problem yesterday. Don't you move now. I'll be right back."

"Okay," said Rashaad, "Just don't take too long."

Mr. Bigalow disappeared into the back room. Rashaad had never been back there. He wondered what was in that room.

Rashaad looked around the barbershop. His daddy was playing dominoes with Mr. Huckabee. Rashaad could hear the slapping of the dominoes on the wooden table.

People were sitting in all ten of the metal folding chairs along the wall. They waited patiently for Mr. Bigalow. Folks knew not to get out of their seats. A new customer would have your seat in no seconds flat.

"Sorry my man, I hope I didn't take too long," called Mr. Bigalow as he came back into the room.

He nonchalantly picked up his clippers and resumed cutting Rashaad's hair.

ZOOOOOOOOOOM!

"Now, what was that word again? I got side tracked when I went to adjust my clippers. Oh, I remember. The word was IDIOSYNCRATIC. It means peculiar or distinctive."

Rashaad and his daddy looked at each other.
His daddy winked.

"That's right," said Rashaad.

"How do you know I'm right?" Mr. Bigalow demanded. "I thought you didn't know this one."

Rashaad looked over at his daddy again.
His daddy smiled.

"Yeah! Uh-huh! I know! Just don't say a word," said Mr. Bigalow, before Rashaad could answer.

"You're finishing up already?" asked Rashaad, trying to look in the mirror behind him.

"I sure am. It don't take me long. Now lay it on me!" Mr. Bigalow said.

"The word is NICHE! What's the meaning?"

"Oh, I know that word. Why, I use it all the time." Mr. Bigalow laughed. "Oh my goodness! I've run out of powder for your neck. I think I've got an extra can on the shelf in the back room. Let me go see. I'll be right back."

Rashaad was getting restless. Suddenly, he remembered that he had money to buy a soft drink out of the machine. Besides, the machine was next to the back room. Rashaad had always wanted to see what was in there.

He got out of the barber's chair. He walked over to the machine. The door to the back room was open just a little.

JACOB
LAWRENCE

STYLES

SHEEN
PRODUCTS

HOW TO
BUILD SO
AIRPLANE
IN ONE
DAY

Rashaad waited ... and waited ... and waited. Mr. Bigalow was taking a long time.

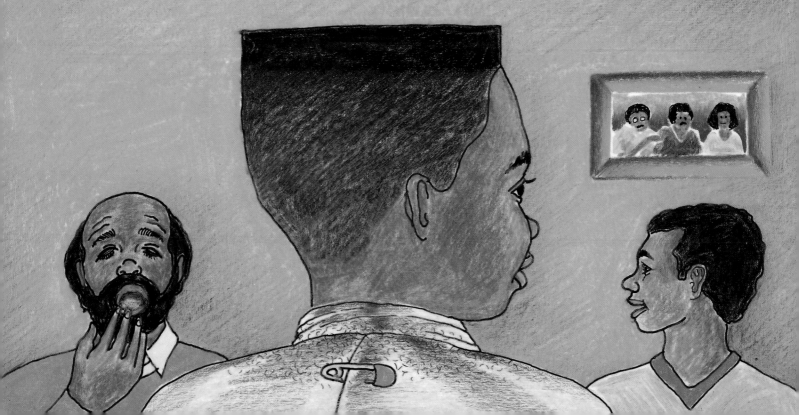

Rashaad pulled the door all the way open. There sat Mr. Bigalow at a little desk. He was looking into the biggest book Rashaad had ever seen.

"Mr. Bigalow!" exclaimed Rashaad.

Mr. Bigalow jumped. The big book went tumbling to the floor.

"Rashaad, what you doin' in here?"

"Mr. Bigalow, you been cheating!"

"My man, this ain't cheating!" said Mr. Bigalow. "I'm doin' what I'm supposed to do. I use the tools of my trade. You want to cut hair like I do, you got to use these clippers. You want to learn words, you got to use the DICTIONARY! I call it my cutting edge."

"Your cutting edge?" asked Rashaad.

"That's right. Like I always say, words are my game, Mr. Bigalow is my name. Now come on outa here. I'll put a little powder around your neck. I got folks waitin' on me."

Rashaad nodded. "Mr. Bigalow, you one cool dude."

The Barber's Cutting Edge

Dedicated to my supportive family, especially my son, Lance Lamont
Lavert, who gave me the idea and the courage to write this book.
With special thanks to Mr. Everett James Fort at the Tex-Ark Barber Shop.
– *Gwendolyn Battle-Lavert*

Dedicated to my mother, Carolyn Holbert. With special
thanks to my wife, Susan DeMersseman; my children,
Lauren Dakota, Brian Jaymes, and Onika; and to barbers like
Mr. Bigalow in every community. – *Raymond Holbert*

Gwedolyn Battle-Lavert is a reading specialist and former elementary school teacher
who lives in Marion, Indiana.

Raymond Holbert is an artist, illustrator, and college art instructor who lives in
Oakland, California.

Story copyright © 1994 by Gwendolyn Battle-Lavert. All rights reserved.
Illustrations copyright © 1994 by Raymond Holbert. All rights reserved.
Editors: Harriet Rohmer and David Schecter
Design: Mira Reisberg   Production: Kristen Zimmerman

Children's Book Press is a nonprofit publisher of multicultural and bilingual literature for children,
supported in part by grants from the California Arts Council. Visit us on the web at **www.childrensbookpress.org**
or, for a complimentary catalog, write to us at: **Children's Book Press, 2211 Mission Street, San Francisco, CA 94110.**

Library of Congress Cataloging-in-Publication Data
Battle-Lavert, Gwendolyn.
    The barber's cutting edge / story by Gwendolyn Battle-Lavert; pictures by Raymond Holbert.
        p.   cm.
    Summary: Rashaad gets his hair cut by the best barber in town who also mentors him on the joy of learning new words.
    ISBN: 0-89239-196-0 [paperback]
    [1. Vocabulary—Fiction. 2. Barbers—Fiction. 3. Afro-Americans—Fiction.] I. Holbert, Raymond, ill. II. Title.
    PZ7.B32446Bar   1994
    [E]—dc20   94-4013   CIP   AC

Printed in Hong Kong through Marwin Productions. Typeset in Stone Informal.
10   9   8   7   6   5   4   3   2   1